Dizzy's Bird Watch

by Alison Inches
illustrated by Cheryl Mendenhall

Ready-to-Read

Simon Spotlight

New York London Toronto Sydney Singapore

Based upon the television series *Bob the Builder*™
created by HIT Entertainment PLC and Keith Chapman,
with thanks to HOT animation, as seen on Nick Jr.®

SIMON SPOTLIGHT
An imprint of Simon & Schuster Children's Publishing Division
1230 Avenue of the Americas, New York, New York 10020

First Edition 10 9 8 7 6 5
Manufactured in the United States of America

Library of Congress Cataloging-in-Publication Data

Inches, Alison
Dizzy's bird watch / by Alison Inches.-1st ed.
p. cm. - (Bob the builder ; 1)
Summary: Bob the builder leaves Dizzy the cement mixer to guard a nest of eggs.
ISBN 0-689-84390-9
[1. Birds-Nests-Fiction. 2. Trucks-Fiction.] I. Title. II. Series.
PZ7.I355 Di 2001
[E]-dc21 2001020178

"I found a bird's NEST!"
said BOB.
"And the NEST has an EGG
in it!"

"This is not a safe place for a NEST," BOB said.
"DIZZY, will you watch the NEST and the MOTHER BIRD?"

"You bet,  BOB!" said 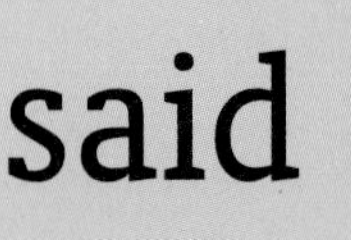  DIZZY.

BOB called the machines.

They had a ROOF to fix.

DIZZY stayed to watch

the EGG.

DIZZY was a good EGG watcher . . . until she kicked her BALL !

Bounce! Bounce!

"Meow!" said PILCHARD.

"Chirp!" said the MOTHER BIRD.

"The NEST!" cried WENDY.

"Oops, that was close!" said WENDY.

"Sorry," said DIZZY.

"Chirp! Chirp!"

WENDY, DIZZY, and PILCHARD looked into the NEST.

The EGG had hatched!

The BABY BIRD grew and grew.
But it was not ready to
leave the NEST.

DIZZY helped the MOTHER BIRD

and watched the BABY BIRD

in the 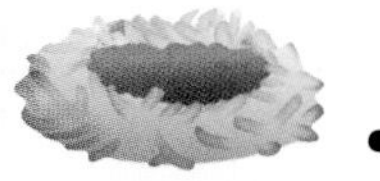 NEST .

One day the BABY BIRD jumped out of the NEST!

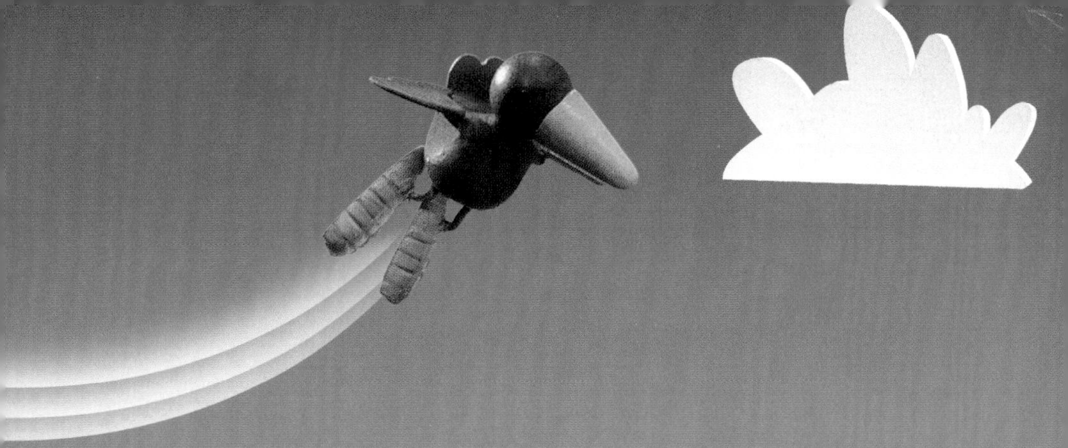

The BABY BIRD flapped its wings.
Then the BABY BIRD flew in
a circle.

The BABY BIRD landed on DIZZY's head.

"Hello, BABY BIRD! I am your Aunt DIZZY!"

"Chirp! Chirp!" said

the BABY BIRD.

"The BABY BIRD is saying thank you for watching the NEST," WENDY said.

DIZZY was so proud. "I am a cement mixer, a BABY BIRD watcher, and an aunt!"

“Hooray for  DIZZY!” said BOB, WENDY, and the team.